You Are the Best Medicine

Julie Aigner Clark

Illustrated by Jana Christy

Balzer + Bray
An Imprint of HarperCollinsPublishers

Balzer + Bray is an imprint of HarperCollins Publishers.

You Are the Best Medicine

Text copyright © 2010 by Julie Aigner Clark

Illustrations copyright © 2010 by Jana Christy

For information address HarperCollins Children's Books, a division of

HarperCollins Publishers, 10 East 53rd Street, New York, NY 10022.

www.harpercollinschildrens.com

Library of Congress Cataloging-in-Publication Data

Aigner-Clark, Julie.

    You are the best medicine / Julie Aigner Clark ; illustrated by Jana Christy. — 1st ed.

        p.   cm.

    Summary: A mother who has cancer gently informs her child of what the effects will

be, and reminds her little one of all the special times they have shared, and will continue to

share, even while she undergoes treatment.

    ISBN 978-0-06-195644-7 (trade bdg.)

    [1. Cancer—Fiction.   2. Mother and child—Fiction.   3. Sick—Fiction.]   I. Christy, Jana,

ill. II. Title.

PZ7.A26927Bes 2010   2009034969

[E]—dc22   CIP

                                                     AC

Typography by Jennifer Rozbruch

10 11 12 13 14 LEO 10 9 8 7 6 5 4 3 2 1
❖
First Edition

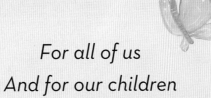

For all of us
And for our children

—Julie

For Debbie Christy

—Jana

When I tell you I have cancer, I will be sad. I will be sad because I am sick, but I will be happy because it is not a sickness that you can catch from me, and so you can still kiss me and hug me and love me.

And you will light up my whole room with your big smile when I am resting. Then I will remember the first time you smiled.

Though you were only weeks old, I knew
that I would never love anyone in the whole
world more than I loved you, that day that
you first smiled.

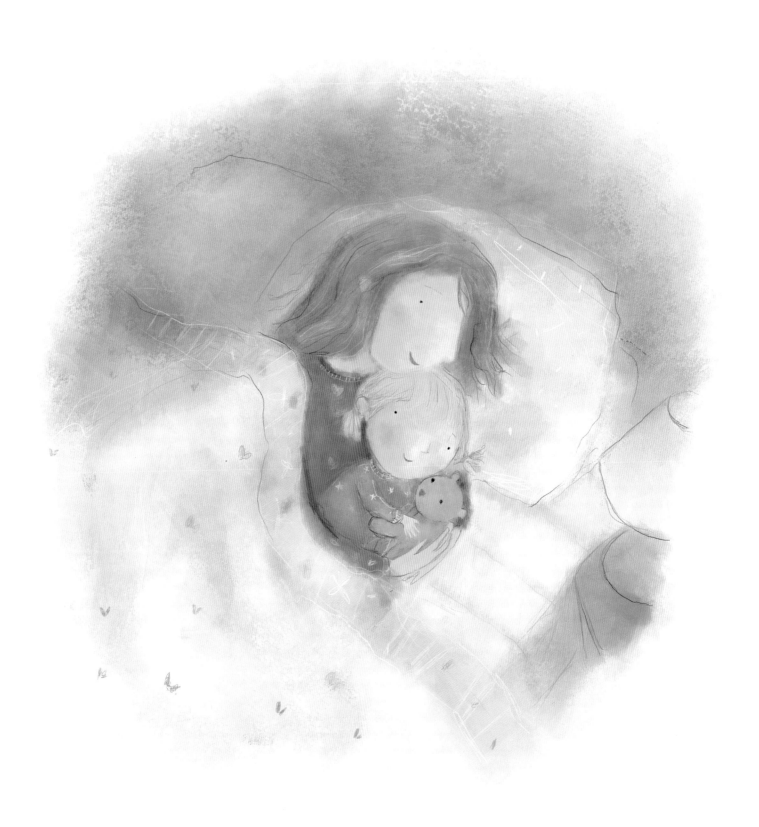

Sometimes I will feel scared, because I have to go to the doctor a lot. But I will remember the times when you were scared, times when you had a nightmare and came into my room to sleep with me. Your skin was as soft as a butterfly's wing, and you curled against me and we felt safe.

And I will be happy because you can still

cocoon with me in my mommy bed and

make me feel sweet and quiet.

For a while I will have to take medicine that makes me feel bad, and this medicine will make all my hair fall out. I will look different.

But I will laugh when I remember your own
sweet little baby head, how round and bald
it was, and how warm it was on my lips
when I kissed it every day.

I will remember how the fuzzy parts grew silky on the top, sticking straight up like little feathers, and how you laughed when I blew raspberries on your round baby belly. I will hope that my new hair grows in as beautifully as yours did.

There will be some days when I don't feel good, and then I will think of all the times I took care of you when you felt sick, and how I brought Popsicles for your sore throat and warm soup with crackers to fill your tummy.

I will be happy when you help me to feel better—when you bring me tea with honey and you sit with me and tell me stories of your day.

When I am getting better, I will often be tired. Then I will think of how you slept so soundly every time you rode in your baby seat in the back of the car.

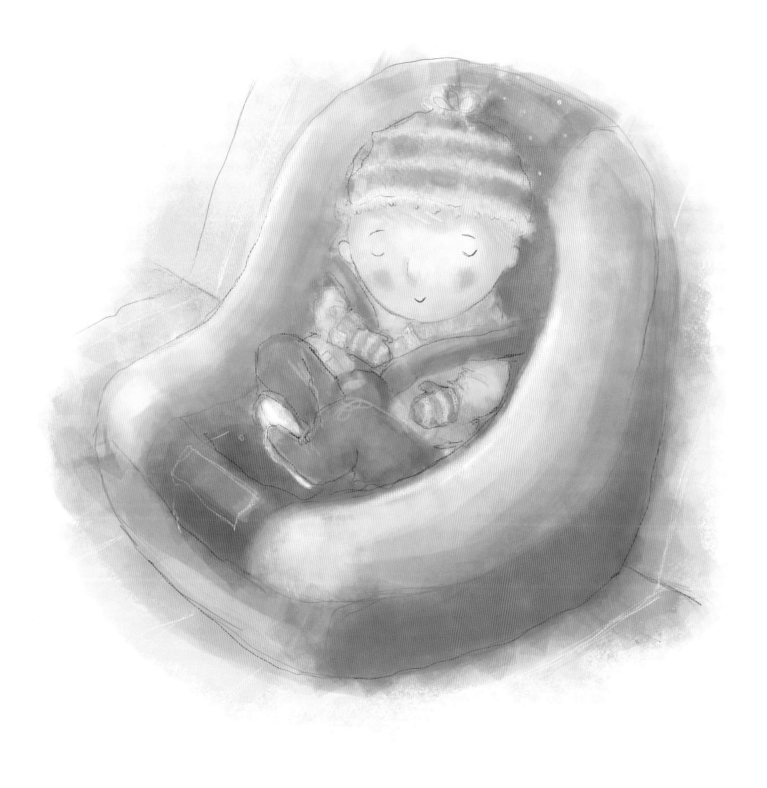

I will remember your still, soft face sleeping

as you curled like a roly-poly bug in your

clean white crib breathing in and out, in and

out, quiet as the moon. I will dream sweet

dreams when I remember these times.

Sometimes I will be sad that I am sick, but then

I will think of how we have laughed and laughed

at our own private jokes, and I will remember

where to tickle you, and how you loved it when

I played this-little-piggy games with your toes.

And then I won't be sad anymore.

And then I will be well. And I will think of all the happiest times that we have had, like birthday parties and swimming and hide-and-go-seek,

and I will think of all
the happy times we are
going to have together
tomorrow,

and the day after that, and the day after that. And we will look back on this time and remember that love and kindness really are the best medicine.